F f

Fred, Me, and the Letter F

Alphabet Friends

by Cynthia Klingel and Robert B. Noyed

The **Child's World**

The Child's World

Published in the United States of America
by The Child's World®
P.O. Box 326
Chanhassen, MN 55317-0326
800-599-READ
www.childsworld.com

The Child's World®: Mary Berendes, Publishing Director

Editorial Directions, Inc.: E. Russell Primm, Editorial
Director; Emily Dolbear, Line Editor; Ruth Martin,
Editorial Assistant; Linda S. Koutris, Photo Researcher
and Selector

Photographs ©: Cover: Cover & 9, 10, 14; Don
Farrall/Photodisc/Getty Images: 13; Yann Arthus-
Bertrand/Corbis: 17; Buddy Mays/Corbis: 18;
Tom Bean/Corbis: 21.

Library of Congress Cataloging-in-Publication Data
Klingel, Cynthia Fitterer.
  Fred, me, and the letter F / by Cynthia Klingel and
Robert B. Noyed.
    p. cm. — (Alphabet readers)
Summary: A simple story about a boy and his friend
Fred and the camping trip they take introduces the
letter "f".
  ISBN 1-59296-096-0 (alk. paper)
[1. Camping—Fiction. 2. Alphabet.] I. Noyed, Robert
B. II. Title. III. Series.
  PZ7.K6798Fr 2003
  [E]—dc21   2003006533

Note to parents and educators:

The first skill children acquire before becoming successful readers is individual letter recognition. The Alphabet Friends series has been created with the needs of young learners in mind. Each engaging book begins by showing the difference between the capital letter and the lowercase letter. In each of the books on the vowels and the consonants c and g, children are introduced to the different sounds that the letter can make. Finally, children see that the letters can be found at the beginning of a word, in the middle of a word, and in most cases, at the end of a word.

Following the introduction, children meet their Alphabet Friends. The friend in each story encounters many words that include the featured letter of that book. Each noun that begins with the title letter is highlighted in red with the initial letter of the word in bold. Above the word is a rebus drawing that establishes a strong picture cue.

At the end of each book, we have included three words lists. Can your young learners find all the words in each book with the title letter in them?

Let's learn about the letter **F.**

The letter **F** can look like this: **F**.

The letter **F** can also look like this: **f.**

The letter **f** can be at the beginning of a word, like fish.

fish

The letter **f** can be in the middle of a word, like giraffe.

gira**ff**e

The letter **f** can be at the

end of a word, like calf.

cal**f**

I went camping with my friend Fred.

Fred caught a fat fish. He wanted to fry

his fish for supper.

Fred and I found a frog. The frog

jumped away. The frog was too fast

for Fred.

Fred found some feathers from a bird.

We felt the feathers. The feathers were

soft and fuzzy.

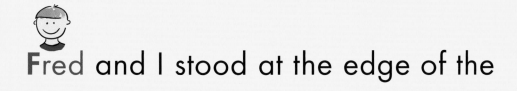

Fred and I stood at the edge of the

forest. We were looking for furry animals.

Finally, we saw a **f**amily of deer!

15

Fred and I were afraid of the deer. We

ran away from the **f**amily of fighting deer.

17

Fred and I felt very hungry. We left

the forest to find some food. Dad fried

the fish over the fire. My friend Fred

and I ate the fried fish.

We ended our fun day in front of the fire.

Now it is time to fall asleep. I am looking

forward to flapjacks for breakfast!

Fun Facts

 There are more than 25,000 species, or kinds, of fish! Scientists discover hundreds of new species each year. The largest fish in the world is the whale shark. Whale sharks weigh more than elephants! The smallest fish is less than an inch (2.54 centimeters) long when fully grown.

 Did you know that flapjacks is another name for pancakes? People have been making pancakes for at least 300 years. They have been made in many different ways and called by many different names, including johnnycakes and slapjacks. French, Russian, and Native American peoples all have their own versions of the flapjack.

 Frogs are amphibians. Most amphibians live both in water and on land. Frogs are born in the water and live there as tadpoles. When they grow older, they move to land. Frogs live on every continent except Antarctica. One kind of frog in Africa can grow to be 16 inches (30 to 40 cm) long. That's longer than this book!

To Read More

About the Letter F

Flanagan, Alice K. *Four Fish: The Sound of F.* Chanhassen, Minn.: The Child's World, 2000.

About Fish

Dr. Seuss. *One Fish, Two Fish, Red Fish, Blue Fish.* New York: Random House, 1960.

Pfister, Marcus. *Rainbow Fish A, B, C.* New York: North-South Books, 2002.

About Flapjacks

Minarik, Else Holmelund, and David T. Wenzel (illustrator). *Father's Flying Flapjacks.* New York: HarperFestival, 2002.

Numeroff, Laura Joffe, and Felicia Bond (illustrator). *If You Give a Pig a Pancake.* New York: Laura Geringer Books, 1998.

About Frogs

Bentley, Dawn, and Salina Yoon (illustrator). *The Icky Sticky Frog.* Santa Monica, Calif.: Piggy Toes Press, 1999.

London, Jonathan, and Frank Remkiewicz (illustrator). *Froggy Bakes a Cake.* New York: Grosset and Dunlap, 2000.

Words with F

Words with F at the Beginning

fall
family
fast
fat
feathers
felt
fighting
finally
find
fire
fish
flapjacks
food
for
forest
forward
found
Fred
fried
friend
frog
from
front
fry
fun
furry
fuzzy

Words with F in the Middle

afraid
breakfast
giraffe
left
soft

Words with F at the End

calf
of

About the Authors

Cynthia Klingel has worked as a high school English teacher and an elementary teacher. She is currently the curriculum director for a Minnesota school district. Cynthia Klingel lives with her family in Mankato, Minnesota.

Robert B. Noyed started his career as a newspaper reporter. Since then, he has worked in communications and public relations for a Minnesota school district for more than fourteen years. Robert B. Noyed lives with his family in Brooklyn Center, Minnesota.